TULSA CITY-COUNTY LIBRARY

MREP

W9-AGM-435

Presented to
Tulsa City-County Library
by the

Anne V. Zarrow Library Books for Children Fund

Tulsa Community Foundation

tulsa
LIBRARY TRUST

APR -- 2023

LOU

Breanna Carzoo

HARPER
An Imprint of HarperCollins*Publishers*

Lou
Copyright © 2022 by Breanna Carzoo
All rights reserved. Manufactured in Italy.
No part of this book may be used or reproduced in any manner whatsoever without written permission except in the case of brief quotations embodied in critical articles and reviews. For information address HarperCollins Children's Books, a division of HarperCollins Publishers, 195 Broadway, New York, NY 10007.
www.harpercollinschildrens.com

ISBN 978-0-06-305405-9

22 23 24 25 26 RTLO 10 9 8 7 6 5 4 3 2
❖
First Edition

To Chris, for seeing greatness in me
before I saw it in myself

Hello!

Can you see me down here?

My name is Lou, and I'm...

DOGGY DAY CARE
OLIVER'S TOYS

a toilet.

All day,
every day,
one by one...

they **SNIFF**

and **TWIRL**

and **TWIST**

and **LIFT**

and...

well, you know.

I know I'm useful.

It's just that sometimes...

deep down inside,

I feel like there's more in me than what they can see.

Like I'm full of greatness!

I just don't know what it is

or how to let it out.

And can I tell you something?
Just between you and me?

I worry sometimes.

What if this is all I am? All I'll ever be?

What if I never do anything more...

...important?

Oh no, here we go again.

One by one, they...

SNIFF and

Uh, do I see smoke?

TWIRL and

Wait! What's going on?

TWIST and
Whoa, that feels really weird.
LIFT!

Ah! Why's everyone looking at me?

Oh! I see it now!
I know what I have to do!

WHOA!

WHOOSH!
OLIVER'S
CARE
WOO HOO!

How did I not see this before?
My name is Lou, and I'm...

DOGGY DAY CARE
OLIVER'S TOYS

a superhero!